The Point of View

Henry James

Contents

THE POINT OF VIEW

BY

Henry James

I. FROM MISS AURORA CHURCH, AT SEA, TO MISS WHITESIDE, IN PARIS.

. . . My dear child, the bromide of sodium (if that's what you call it) proved perfectly useless. I don't mean that it did me no good, but that I never had occasion to take the bottle out of my bag. It might have done wonders for me if I had needed it; but I didn't, simply because I have been a wonder myself. Will you believe that I have spent the whole voyage on deck, in the most animated conversation and exercise? Twelve times round the deck make a mile, I believe; and by this measurement I have been walking twenty miles a day. And down to every meal, if you please, where I have displayed the appetite of a fish-wife. Of course the weather has been lovely; so there's no great merit. The wicked old Atlantic has been as blue as the sapphire in my only ring (a rather good one), and as smooth as the slippery floor of Madame Galopin's dining-room. We have been for the last three hours in sight of land, and we are soon to enter the Bay of New York, which is said to be exquisitely beautiful. But of course you recall it, though they say that everything changes so fast over here. I find I don't remember anything, for my recollections of our voyage to Europe, so many years ago, are exceedingly dim; I only have a painful impression that mamma shut me up for an hour every day in the state-room, and made me learn by heart some religious poem. I was only five years old, and I believe that as a child I was extremely timid; on the other hand, mamma, as you know, was dreadfully severe. She is severe to this day; only I have become indifferent; I have been so pinched and pushed--morally speaking, bien entendu. It is true, however, that there are children of five on the vessel today who have been extremely conspicuous--ranging all over the ship, and always under one's feet. Of course they are little compatriots, which means that they are little barbarians. I don't mean that all our compatriots are barbarous; they seem to improve, somehow, after their first

communion. I don't know whether it's that ceremony that improves them, especially as so few of them go in for it; but the women are certainly nicer than the little
girls; I mean, of course, in proportion, you know. You warned me not to generalise,
and you see I have already begun, before we have arrived. But I suppose there is no
harm in it so long as it is favourable. Isn't it favourable when I say that I have had
the most lovely time? I have never had so much liberty in my life, and I have been
out alone, as you may say, every day of the voyage. If it is a foretaste of what is to
come, I shall take to that very kindly. When I say that I have been out alone, I
mean that we have always been two. But we two were alone, so to speak, and it was
not like always having mamma, or Madame Galopin, or some lady in the pension,
or the temporary cook. Mamma has been very poorly; she is so very well on land,
it's a wonder to see her at all taken down. She says, however, that it isn't the being
at sea; it's, on the contrary, approaching the land. She is not in a hurry to arrive; she
says that great disillusions await us. I didn't know that she had any illusions--she's
so stern, so philosophic. She is very serious; she sits for hours in perfect silence,
with her eyes fixed on the horizon. I heard her say yesterday to an English gentle-
man--a very odd Mr. Antrobus, the only person with whom she converses--that she
was afraid she shouldn't like her native land, and that she shouldn't like not liking
it. But this is a mistake--she will like that immensely (I mean not liking it). If it
should prove at all agreeable, mamma will be furious, for that will go against her
system. You know all about mamma's system; I have explained that so often. It
goes against her system that we should come back at all; that was MY system--I
have had at last to invent one! She consented to come only because she saw that,
having no dot, I should never marry in Europe; and I pretended to be immensely
pre-occupied with this idea, in order to make her start. In reality cela m'est parfait-
ement egal. I am only afraid I shall like it too much (I don't mean marriage, of
course, but one's native land). Say what you will, it's a charming thing to go out
alone, and I have given notice to mamma that I mean to be always en course. When
I tell her that, she looks at me in the same silence; her eye dilates, and then she
slowly closes it. It's as if the sea were affecting her a little, though it's so beauti-
fully calm. I ask her if she will try my bromide, which is there in my bag; but she
motions me off, and I begin to walk again, tapping my little boot-soles upon the
smooth clean deck. This allusion to my boot-soles, by the way, is not prompted by

vanity; but it's a fact that at sea one's feet and one's shoes assume the most extraordinary importance, so that we should take the precaution to have nice ones. They are all you seem to see as the people walk about the deck; you get to know them intimately, and to dislike some of them so much. I am afraid you will think that I have already broken loose; and for aught I know, I am writing as a demoiselle bien-elevee should not write. I don't know whether it's the American air; if it is, all I can say is that the American air is very charming. It makes me impatient and restless, and I sit scribbling here because I am so eager to arrive, and the time passes better if I occupy myself. I am in the saloon, where we have our meals, and opposite to me is a big round porthole, wide open, to let in the smell of the land. Every now and then I rise a little and look through it, to see whether we are arriving. I mean in the Bay, you know, for we shall not come up to the city till dark. I don't want to lose the Bay; it appears that it's so wonderful. I don't exactly understand what it contains, except some beautiful islands; but I suppose you will know all about that. It is easy to see that these are the last hours, for all the people about me are writing letters to put into the post as soon as we come up to the dock. I believe they are dreadful at the custom-house, and you will remember how many new things you persuaded mamma that (with my pre-occupation of marriage) I should take to this country, where even the prettiest girls are expected not to go unadorned. We ruined ourselves in Paris (that is part of mamma's solemnity); mais au moins je serai belle! Moreover, I believe that mamma is prepared to say or to do anything that may be necessary for escaping from their odious duties; as she very justly remarks, she can't afford to be ruined twice. I don't know how one approaches these terrible douaniers, but I mean to invent something very charming. I mean to say, "Voyons, Messieurs, a young girl like me, brought up in the strictest foreign traditions, kept always in the background by a very superior mother--la voila; you can see for yourself!--what is it possible that she should attempt to smuggle in? Nothing but a few simple relics of her convent!" I won't tell them that my convent was called the Magasin du Bon Marche. Mamma began to scold me three days ago for insisting on so many trunks, and the truth is that, between us, we have not fewer than seven. For relics, that's a good many! We are all writing very long letters--or at least we are writing a great number. There is no news of the Bay as yet. Mr. Antrobus, mamma's friend, opposite to me, is beginning on his ninth. He is an Honourable, and a Member of Parliament; he has written, during the voyage, about a hundred letters, and he seems greatly alarmed at the number of stamps he will have to buy when he arrives. He is full of information; but he has not enough, for he asks as many questions as mamma when she goes to hire apartments. He is going to "look into" various things; he speaks as if they had a little hole for the purpose. He walks almost as much as I, and he has very big shoes. He asks questions even of me, and I tell him again and again that I know nothing about America. But it makes no difference; he always begins again, and, indeed, it is not strange that he should find my ignorance incredible. "Now, how would it be in one of your South-Western States?"--that's his favourite way of opening conversation. Fancy me giving an account of the South- Western States! I tell him he had better ask mamma--a little to tease that lady, who knows no more about such places than I. Mr. Antrobus is very big and black; he speaks with a sort of brogue; he has a wife and ten children; he is not very romantic. But he has lots of letters to people la-bas (I forget that we are just arriving), and mamma, who takes an interest in him in spite of his views (which are dreadfully advanced, and not at all like mamma's own), has promised to give him the entree to the best society. I don't know what she knows about the best society over here today, for we have not kept up our connections at all, and no one will know (or, I am afraid, care) anything about us. She has an idea that we shall be immensely recognised; but really, except the poor little Rucks, who are bankrupt, and, I am told, in no society at all, I don't know on whom we can count. C'est egal. Mamma has an idea that, whether or not we appreciate America ourselves, we shall at least be universally appreciated. It's true that we have begun to be, a little; you would see that by the way that Mr. Cockerel and Mr. Louis Leverett are always inviting me to walk. Both of these gentlemen, who are Americans, have asked leave to call upon me in New York, and I have said, Mon Dieu, oui, if it's the custom of the country. Of course I have not dared to tell this to mamma, who flatters herself that we have brought with us in our trunks a complete set of customs of our own, and that we shall only have to shake them out a little and put them on when we arrive. If only the two gentlemen I just spoke of don't call at the same time, I don't think I shall be too much frightened. If they do, on the other hand, I won't answer for it. They have a particular aversion to each other, and they are ready to fight about poor little me. I am only the pretext, however; for, as Mr. Leverett says, it's really the opposition of temperaments. I hope they won't cut each other's throats, for I am not crazy about either of them. They are very well for the deck of a ship, but I shouldn't care about them in a salon; they are not at all distinguished. They think they are, but they are not; at least Mr. Louis Leverett does; Mr. Cockerel doesn't appear to care so much. They are extremely different (with their opposed temperaments), and each very amusing for a while; but I should get dreadfully tired of passing my life with either. Neither has proposed that, as yet; but it is evidently what they are coming to. It will be in a great measure to spite each other, for I think that au fond they don't quite believe in me. If they don't, it's the only point on which they agree. They hate each other awfully; they take such different views. That is, Mr. Cockerel hates Mr. Leverett--he calls him a sickly little ass: he says that his opinions are half affectation, and the other half dyspepsia. Mr. Leverett speaks of Mr. Cockerel as a "strident savage," but he declares he finds him most diverting. He says there is nothing in which we can't find a certain entertainment, if we only look at it in the right way, and that we have no business with either hating or loving; we ought only to strive to understand. To understand is to forgive, he says. That is very pretty, but I don't like the suppression of our affections, though I have no desire to fix mine upon Mr. Leverett. He is very artistic, and talks like an article in some review, he has lived a great deal in Paris, and Mr. Cockerel says that is what has made him such an idiot. That is not complimentary to you, dear Louisa, and still less to your brilliant brother; for Mr. Cockerel explains that he means it (the bad effect of Paris) chiefly of the men. In fact, he means the bad effect of Europe altogether. This, however, is compromising to mamma; and I am afraid there is no doubt that (from what I have told him) he thinks mamma also an idiot. (I am not responsible, you know--I have always wanted to go home.) If mamma knew him, which she doesn't, for she always closes her eyes when I pass on his arm, she would think him disgusting. Mr. Leverett, however, tells me he is nothing to what we shall see yet. He is from Philadelphia (Mr. Cockerel); he insists that we shall go and see Philadelphia, but mamma says she saw it in 1855, and it was then affreux. Mr. Cockerel says that mamma is evidently not familiar with the march of improvement in this country; he speaks of 1855 as if it were a hundred years ago. Mamma says she knows it goes only too fast--it goes so fast that it has time to do nothing well; and then Mr. Cockerel, who, to do him justice, is perfectly good-natured, remarks that she had better wait till she has been ashore and seen the improvements. Mamma rejoins that she sees them from here, the improvements, and that they give her a sinking of the heart. (This little exchange of ideas is carried on through me; they have never spoken to each other.) Mr. Cockerel, as I say, is extremely good-natured, and he carries out what I have heard said about the men in America being very considerate of the women. They evidently listen to them a great deal; they don't contradict them, but it seems to me that this is rather negative. There is very little gallantry in not contradicting one; and it strikes me that there are some things the men don't express. There are others on the ship whom I've noticed. It's as if they were all one's brothers or one's cousins. But I promised you not to generalise, and perhaps there will be more expression when we arrive. Mr. Cockerel returns to America, after a general tour, with a renewed conviction that this is the only country. I left him on deck an hour ago looking at the coast-line with an opera-glass, and saying it was the prettiest thing he had seen in all his tour. When I re-marked that the coast seemed rather low, he said it would be all the easier to get ashore; Mr. Leverett doesn't seem in a hurry to get ashore; he is sitting within sight of me in a corner of the saloon--writing letters, I suppose, but looking, from the way he bites his pen and rolls his eyes about, as if he were composing a sonnet and waiting for a rhyme. Perhaps the sonnet is addressed to me; but I forget that he suppresses the affections! The only person in whom mamma takes much interest is the great French critic, M. Lejaune, whom we have the honour to carry with us. We have read a few of his works, though mamma disapproves of his tendencies and thinks him a dreadful materialist. We have read them for the style; you know he is one of the new Academicians. He is a Frenchman like any other, except that he is rather more quiet; and he has a gray mustache and the ribbon of the Legion of Honour. He is the first French writer of distinction who has been to America since De Tocqueville; the French, in such matters, are not very enterprising. Also, he has the air of wondering what he is doing dans cette galere. He has come with his beau-frere, who is an engineer, and is looking after some mines, and he talks with scarcely any one else, as he speaks no English, and appears to take for granted that no one speaks French. Mamma would be delighted to assure him of the contrary; she has never conversed with an Academician. She always makes a little vague inclination, with a smile, when he passes her, and he answers with a most respectful bow; but it goes no farther, to mamma's disappointment. He is always with the beau-frere, a rather untidy, fat, bearded man, decorated, too, always smoking and looking at the feet of the ladies, whom mamma (though she has very good feet) has not the courage to aborder. I believe M. Lejaune is going to write a book about America, and Mr. Leverett says it will be terrible. Mr. Leverett has made his acquaintance, and says M. Lejaune will put him into his book; he says the movement of the French intellect is superb. As a general thing, he doesn't care for Academicians, but he thinks M. Lejaune is an exception, he is so living, so personal. I asked Mr. Cockerel what he thought of M. Lejaune's plan of writing a book, and he answered that he didn't see what it mattered to him that a Frenchman the more should make a monkey of himself. I asked him why he hadn't written a book about Europe, and he said that, in the first place, Europe isn't worth writing about, and, in the second, if he said what he thought, people would think it was a joke. He said they are very superstitious about Europe over here; he wants people in America to behave as if Europe didn't exist. I told this to Mr. Leverett, and he answered that if Europe didn't exist America wouldn't, for Europe keeps us alive by buying our corn. He said, also, that the trouble with America in the future will be that she will produce things in such enormous quantities that there won't be enough people in the rest of the world to buy them, and that we shall be left with our productions--most of them very hideous--on our hands. I asked him if he thought corn a hideous production, and he replied that there is nothing more unbeautiful than too much food. I think that to feed the world too well, however, that will be, after all, a beau role. Of course I don't understand these things, and I don't believe Mr. Leverett does; but Mr. Cockerel seems to know what he is talking about, and he says that America is complete in herself. I don't know exactly what he means, but he speaks as if human affairs had somehow moved over to this side of the world. It may be a very good place for them, and Heaven knows I am extremely tired of Europe, which mamma has always insisted so on my appreciating; but I don't think I like the idea of our being so completely cut off. Mr. Cockerel says it is not we that are cut off, but Europe, and he seems to think that Europe has deserved it somehow. That may be; our life over there was sometimes extremely tiresome, though mamma says it is now that our real fatigues will begin. I like to abuse those dreadful old countries myself, but I am not sure that I am pleased when others do the same. We had some rather pretty moments there, after all; and at Piacenza we certainly lived on four francs a day. Mamma is already in a terrible state of mind about the expenses here; she is frightened by what people on the ship (the few that she has spoken to) have told her. There is one comfort, at any rate--we have spent so much money in coming here that we shall have none left to get away. I am scribbling along, as you see, to occupy me till we get news of the islands. Here comes Mr. Cockerel to bring it. Yes, they are in sight; he tells me that they are lovelier than ever, and that I must come right up right away. I suppose you will think that I am already beginning to use the language of the country. It is certain that at the end of a month I shall speak nothing else. I have picked up every dialect, wherever we have travelled; you have heard my Platt-Deutsch and my Neapolitan. But, voyons un peu the Bay! I have just called to Mr. Leverett to remind him of the islands. "The islands--the islands? Ah, my dear young lady, I have seen Capri, I have seen Ischia!" Well, so have I, but that doesn't prevent . . . (A little later.)--I have seen the islands; they are rather queer.

II. MRS. CHURCH, IN NEW YORK, TO MADAME GALOPIN, AT GENEVA.

October 17, 1880.

If I felt far away from you in the middle of that deplorable Atlantic, chere Madame, how do I feel now, in the heart of this extraordinary city? We have arrived,--we have arrived, dear friend; but I don't know whether to tell you that I consider that an advantage. If we had been given our choice of coming safely to land or going down to the bottom of the sea, I should doubtless have chosen the former course; for I hold, with your noble husband, and in opposition to the general tendency of modern thought, that our lives are not our own to dispose of, but a sacred trust from a higher power, by whom we shall be held responsible. Nevertheless, if I had foreseen more vividly some of the impressions that awaited me here, I am not sure that, for my daughter at least, I should not have preferred on the spot to hand in our account. Should I not have been less (rather than more) guilty in presuming to dispose of HER destiny, than of my own? There is a nice point for dear M. Galopin to settle--one of those points which I have heard him discuss in the pulpit with such elevation. We are safe, however, as I say; by which I mean that we are physically safe. We have taken up the thread of our familiar pension-life, but under strikingly different conditions. We have found a refuge in a boarding-house which has been highly recommended to me, and where the arrangements partake of that barbarous magnificence which in this country is the only alternative from primitive rudeness. The terms, per week, are as magnificent as all the rest. The landlady wears diamond ear- rings; and the drawing-rooms are decorated with marble statues. I should indeed be sorry to let you know how I have allowed myself to be ranconnee; and I--should be still more sorry that it should come to the ears of any of my good friends in Geneva, who know me less well than you and might judge me more harshly.

There is no wine given for dinner, and I have vainly requested the person who conducts the establishment to garnish her table more liberally. She says I may have all the wine I want if I will order it at the merchant's, and settle the matter with him. But I have never, as you know, consented to regard our modest allowance of eau rougie as an extra; indeed, I remember that it is largely to your excellent advice that I have owed my habit of being firm on this point. There are, however, greater difficulties than the question of what we shall drink for dinner, chere Madame. Still, I have never lost courage, and I shall not lose courage now. At the worst, we can re- embark again, and seek repose and refreshment on the shores of your beautiful lake. (There is absolutely no scenery here!) We shall not, perhaps, in that case have achieved what we desired, but we shall at least have made an honourable retreat. What we desire--I know it is just this that puzzles you, dear friend; I don't think you ever really comprehended my motives in taking this formidable step, though you were good enough, and your magnanimous husband was good enough, to press my hand at parting in a way that seemed to say that you would still be with me, even if I was wrong. To be very brief, I wished to put an end to the reclamations of my daughter. Many Americans had assured her that she was wasting her youth in those historic lands which it was her privilege to see so intimately, and this unfortunate conviction had taken possession of her. "Let me at least see for myself," she used to say; "if I should dislike it over there as much as you promise me, so much the better for you. In that case we will come back and make a new arrangement at Stuttgart." The experiment is a terribly expensive one; but you know that my devotion never has shrunk from an ordeal. There is another point, moreover, which, from a mother to a mother, it would be affectation not to touch upon. I remember the just satisfaction with which you announced to me the betrothal of your charming Cecile. You know with what earnest care my Aurora has been educated,--how thoroughly she is acquainted with the principal results of modern research. We have always studied together; we have always enjoyed together. It will perhaps surprise you to hear that she makes these very advantages a reproach to me,--represents them as an injury to herself. "In this country," she says, "the gentlemen have not those accomplishments; they care nothing for the results of modern research; and it will not help a young person to be sought in marriage that she can give an account of the last German theory of Pessimism." That is possible; and I have never concealed from her that it was not for this country that I had educated her. If she marries in the United States it is, of course, my intention that my son-in-law shall accompany us to Europe. But, when she calls my attention more and more to these facts, I feel that we are moving in a different world. This is more and more the country of the many; the few find less and less place for them; and the individual--well, the individual has quite ceased to be recognised. He is recognised as a voter, but he is not recognised as a gentleman--still less as a lady. My daughter and I, of course, can only pretend to constitute a FEW! You know that I have never for a moment remitted my pretensions as an individual, though among the agitations of pension-life, I have sometimes needed all my energy to uphold them. "Oh, yes, I may be poor," I have had occasion to say, "I may be unprotected, I may be reserved, I may occupy a small apartment in the quatrieme, and be unable to scatter unscrupulous bribes among the domestics; but at least I am a PERSON, with personal rights." In this country the people have rights, but the person has none. You would have perceived that if you had come with me to make arrangements at this establishment. The very fine lady who condescends to preside over it kept me waiting twenty minutes, and then came sailing in without a word of apology. I had sat very silent, with my eyes on the clock; Aurora amused herself with a false admiration of the room,--a wonderful drawing-room, with magenta curtains, frescoed walls, and photographs of the landlady's friends--as if one cared anything about her friends! When this exalted personage came in, she simply remarked that she had just been trying on a dress--that it took so long to get a skirt to hang. "It seems to take very long indeed!" I answered. "But I hope the skirt is right at last. You might have sent for us to come up and look at it!" She evidently didn't understand, and when I asked her to show us her rooms, she handed us over to a negro as degingande as herself. While we looked at them I heard her sit down to the piano in the drawing-room; she began to sing an air from a comic opera. I began to fear we had gone quite astray; I didn't know in what house we could be, and was only reassured by seeing a Bible in every room. When we came down our musical hostess expressed no hope that the rooms had pleased us, and seemed quite indifferent to our taking them. She would not consent, moreover, to the least diminution, and was inflexible, as I told you, on the subject of wine. When I pushed this point, she was so good as to observe that she didn't keep a cabaret. One is not in the least considered; there is no respect for one's privacy, for one's preferences, for one's reserves. The familiarity is without limits, and I have already made a dozen acquaintances, of whom I know, and wish to know, nothing. Aurora tells me that she is the "belle of the boarding- house." It appears that this is a great distinction. It brings me back to my poor child and her prospects. She takes a very critical view of them herself: she tells me that I have given her a false education, and that no one will marry her today. No American will marry her, because she is too much of a foreigner, and no foreigner will marry her because she is too much of an American. I remind her that scarcely a day passes that a foreigner, usually of distinction, doesn't select an American bride, and she answers me that in these cases the young lady is not married for her fine eyes. Not always, I reply; and then she declares that she would marry no foreigner who should not be one of the first of the first. You will say, doubtless, that she should content herself with advantages that have not been deemed insufficient for Cecile; but I will not repeat to you the remark she made when I once made use of this argument. You will doubtless be surprised to hear that I have ceased to argue; but it is time I should tell you that I have at last agreed to let her act for herself. She is to live for three months a l'Americaine, and I am to be a mere spectator. You will feel with me that this is a cruel position for a coeur de mere. I count the days till our three months are over, and I know that you will join with me in my prayers. Aurora walks the streets alone. She goes out in the tramway; a voiture de place costs five francs for the least little course. (I beseech you not to let it be known that I have sometimes had the weakness . . .) My daughter is sometimes accompanied by a gentleman--by a dozen gentlemen; she remains out for hours, and her conduct excites no surprise in this establishment. I know but too well the emotions it will excite in your quiet home. If you betray us, chere Madame, we are lost; and why, after all, should any one know of these things in Geneva? Aurora pretends that she has been able to persuade herself that she doesn't care who knows them; but there is a strange expression in her face, which proves that her conscience is not at rest. I watch her, I let her go, but I sit with my hands clasped. There is a peculiar custom in this country-- I shouldn't know how to express it in Genevese--it is called "being attentive," and young girls are the object of the attention. It has not necessarily anything to do with projects of marriage--though it is the privilege only of the unmarried, and though, at the same time (fortunately, and this may surprise you) it has no relation to other projects. It is simply an invention by which young persons of the two sexes pass their time together. How shall I muster courage to tell you that Aurora is now engaged in this delassement, in company with several gentlemen? Though it has no relation to marriage, it happily does not exclude it, and marriages have been known to take place in consequence (or in spite) of it. It is true that even in this country a young lady may marry but one husband at a time, whereas she may receive at once the attentions of several gentlemen, who are equally entitled "admirers." My daughter, then, has admirers to an indefinite number. You will think I am joking, perhaps, when I tell you that I am unable to be exact--I who was formerly l'exactitude meme. Two of these gentlemen are, to a certain extent, old friends, having been passengers on the steamer which carried us so far from you. One of them, still young, is typical of the American character, but a respectable person, and a lawyer in considerable practice. Every one in this country follows a profession; but it must be admitted that the professions are more highly remunerated than chez vous. Mr. Cockerel, even while I write you, is in complete possession of my daughter. He called for her an hour ago in a "boghey,"--a strange, unsafe, rickety vehicle, mounted on enormous wheels, which holds two persons very near together; and I watched her from the window take her place at his side. Then he whirled her away, behind two little horses with terribly thin legs; the whole equipage--and most of all her being in it--was in the most questionable taste. But she will return, and she will return very much as she went. It is the same when she goes down to Mr. Louis Leverett, who has no vehicle, and who merely comes and sits with her in the front salon. He has lived a great deal in Europe, and is very fond of the arts, and though I am not sure I agree with him in his views of the relation of art to life and life to art, and in his interpretation of some of the great works that Aurora and I have studied together, he seems to me a sufficiently serious and intelligent young man. I do not regard him as intrinsically dangerous; but on the other hand, he offers absolutely no guarantees. I have no means whatever of ascertaining his pecuniary situation. There is a vagueness on these points which is extremely embarrassing, and it never occurs to young men to offer you a reference. In Geneva I should not be at a loss; I should come to you, chere Madame, with my little inquiry, and what you should not be able to tell me would not be worth knowing. But no one in New York can give me the smallest information about the etat de fortune of Mr. Louis Leverett. It is true that he is a native of Boston, where most of his friends reside; I cannot, however, go to the expense of a journey to Boston simply to learn, perhaps, that Mr. Leverett (the young Louis) has an income of five thousand francs. As I say, however, he does not strike me as dangerous. When Aurora comes back to me, after having passed an hour with the young Louis, she says that he has described to her his emotions on visiting the home of Shelley, or discussed some of the differences between the Boston Temperament and that of the Italians of the Renaissance. You will not enter into these rapprochements, and I can't blame you. But you won't betray me, chere Madame?

III. FROM MISS STURDY, AT NEWPORT,
TO MRS. DRAPER, IN FLORENCE.

September 30.

I promised to tell you how I like it, but the truth is, I have gone to and fro so often that I have ceased to like and dislike. Nothing strikes me as unexpected; I expect everything in its order. Then, too, you know, I am not a critic; I have no talent for keen analysis, as the magazines say; I don't go into the reasons of things. It is true I have been for a longer time than usual on the wrong side of the water, and I admit that I feel a little out of training for American life. They are breaking me in very fast, however. I don't mean that they bully me; I absolutely decline to be bullied. I say what I think, because I believe that I have, on the whole, the advantage of knowing what I think--when I think anything--which is half the battle. Sometimes, indeed, I think nothing at all. They don't like that over here; they like you to have impressions. That they like these impressions to be favourable appears to me perfectly natural; I don't make a crime to them of that; it seems to me, on the contrary, a very amiable quality. When individuals have it, we call them sympathetic; I don't see why we shouldn't give nations the same benefit. But there are things I haven't the least desire to have an opinion about. The privilege of indifference is the dearest one we possess, and I hold that intelligent people are known by the way they exercise it. Life is full of rubbish, and we have at least our share of it over here. When you wake up in the morning you find that during the night a cartload has been deposited in your front garden. I decline, however, to have any of it in my premises; there are thousands of things I want to know nothing about. I have outlived the necessity of being hypocritical; I have nothing to gain and everything to lose. When one is fifty years old--single, stout, and red in the face--one has outlived a good many necessities. They tell me over here that my increase of weight is extremely marked, and though they don't tell me that I am coarse, I am sure they think me so. There is very little coarseness here--not quite enough, I think--though there is plenty of vulgarity, which is a very different thing. On the whole, the country is becoming much more agreeable. It isn't that the people are charming, for that they always were (the best of them, I mean, for it isn't true of the others), but that places and things as well have acquired the art of pleasing. The houses are extremely good, and they look so extraordinarily fresh and clean. European interiors, in comparison, seem musty and gritty. We have a great deal of taste; I shouldn't wonder if we should end by inventing something pretty; we only need a little time. Of course, as yet, it's all imitation, except, by the way, these piazzas. I am sitting on one now; I am writing to you with my portfolio on my knees. This broad light loggia surrounds the house with a movement as free as the expanded wings of a bird, and the wandering airs come up from the deep sea, which murmurs on the rocks at the end of the lawn. Newport is more charming even than you remember it; like everything else over here, it has improved. It is very exquisite today; it is, indeed, I think, in all the world, the only exquisite watering-place, for I detest the whole genus. The crowd has left it now, which makes it all the better, though plenty of talkers remain in these large, light, luxurious houses, which are planted with a kind of Dutch definiteness all over the green carpet of the cliff. This carpet is very neatly laid and wonderfully well swept, and the sea, just at hand, is capable of prodigies of blue. Here and there a pretty woman strolls over one of the lawns, which all touch each other, you know, without hedges or fences; the light looks intense as it plays upon her brilliant dress; her large parasol shines like a silver dome. The long lines of the far shores are soft and pure, though they are places that one hasn't the least desire to visit. Altogether the effect is very delicate, and anything that is delicate counts immensely over here; for delicacy, I think, is as rare as coarseness. I am talking to you of the sea, however, without having told you a word of my voyage. It was very comfortable and amusing; I should like to take another next month. You know I am almost offensively well at sea--that I breast the weather and brave the storm. We had no storm fortunately, and I had brought with me a supply of light literature; so I passed nine days on deck in my sea-chair, with my heels up, reading Tauchnitz novels. There was a great lot of people, but no one in particular, save some fifty American girls. You know all about the American girl, however, having been one yourself. They are, on the whole, very nice, but fifty is too many; there are always too many. There was an inquiring Briton, a radical M.P., by name Mr. Antrobus, who entertained me as much as any one else. He is an excellent man; I even asked him to come down here and spend a couple of days. He looked rather frightened, till I told him he shouldn't be alone with me, that the house was my brother's, and that I gave the invitation in his name. He came a week ago; he goes everywhere; we have heard of him in a dozen places. The English are very simple, or at least they seem so over here. Their old measurements and comparisons desert them; they don't know whether it's all a joke, or whether it's too serious by half. We are quicker than they, though we talk so much more slowly. We think fast, and yet we talk as deliberately as if we were speaking a foreign language. They toss off their sentences with an air of easy familiarity with the tongue, and yet they misunderstand two-thirds of what people say to them. Perhaps, after all, it is only OUR thoughts they think slowly; they think their own often to a lively tune enough. Mr. Antrobus arrived here at eight o'clock in the morning; I don't know how he managed it; it appears to be his favourite hour; wherever we have heard of him he has come in with the dawn. In England he would arrive at 5.30 p.m. He asks innumerable questions, but they are easy to answer, for he has a sweet credulity. He made me rather ashamed; he is a better American than so many of us; he takes us more seriously than we take ourselves. He seems to think that an oligarchy of wealth is growing up here, and he advised me to be on my guard against it. I don't know exactly what I can do, but I promised him to look out. He is fearfully energetic; the energy of the people here is nothing to that of the inquiring Briton. If we should devote half the energy to building up our institutions that they devote to obtaining information about them, we should have a very satisfactory country. Mr. Antrobus seemed to think very well of us, which surprised me, on the whole, because, say what one will, it's not so agreeable as England. It's very horrid that this should be; and it's delightful, when one thinks of it, that some things in England are, after all, so disagreeable. At the same time, Mr. Antrobus appeared to be a good deal preoccupied with our dangers. I don't understand, quite, what they are; they seem to me so few, on a Newport piazza, on this bright, still day. But, after all, what one sees on a Newport piazza is not America; it's the back of Europe! I don't mean to say that I haven't noticed any dangers since my return; there are two or three that seem to me very serious, but they are not those that Mr. Antrobus means. One, for instance, is that we shall cease to speak the English language, which I prefer so much to any other. It's less and less spoken; American is crowding it out. All the children speak American, and as a child's language it's dreadfully rough. It's exclusively in use in the schools; all the magazines and newspapers are in American. Of course, a people of fifty millions, who have invented a new civilisation, have a right to a language of their own; that's what they tell me, and I can't quarrel with it. But I wish they had made it as pretty as the mother-tongue, from which, after all, it is more or less derived. We ought to have invented something as noble as our country. They tell me it's more expressive, and yet some admirable things have been said in the Queen's English. There can be no question of the Queen over here, of course, and American no doubt is the music of the future. Poor dear future, how "expressive" you'll be! For women and children, as I say, it strikes one as very rough; and moreover, they don't speak it well, their own though it be. My little nephews, when I first came home, had not gone back to school, and it distressed me to see that, though they are charming children, they had the vocal inflections of little news-boys. My niece is sixteen years old; she has the sweetest nature possible; she is extremely well-bred, and is dressed to perfection. She chatters from morning till night; but it isn't a pleasant sound! These little persons are in the opposite case from so many English girls, who know how to speak, but don't know how to talk. My niece knows how to talk, but doesn't know how to speak. A propos of the young people, that is our other danger; the young people are eating us up,--there is nothing in America but the young people. The country is made for the rising generation; life is arranged for them; they are the destruction of society. People talk of them, consider them, defer to them, bow down to them. They are always present, and whenever they are present there is an end to everything else. They are often very pretty; and physically, they are wonderfully looked after; they are scoured and brushed, they wear hygienic clothes, they go every week to the dentist's. But the little boys kick your shins, and the little girls offer to slap your face! There is an immense literature entirely addressed to them, in which the kicking of shins and the slapping of faces is much recommended. As a woman of fifty, I protest. I insist on being judged by my peers. It's too late, however, for several millions of little feet are actively engaged in stamping out conversation, and I don't see how they can long fail to keep it under. The future is theirs; maturity will evidently be at an increasing discount. Longfellow wrote a charming little poem called "The Children's Hour," but he ought to have called it "The Children's Century." And by children, of course, I don't mean simple infants; I mean everything of less than twenty. The social importance of the young American increases steadily up to that age, and then it suddenly stops. The young girls, of course, are more important than the lads; but the lads are very important too. I am struck with the way they are known and talked about; they are little celebrities; they have reputations and pretentions; they are taken very seriously. As for the young girls, as I said just now, there are too many. You will say, perhaps, that I am jealous of them, with my fifty years and my red face. I don't think so, because I don't suffer; my red face doesn't frighten people away, and I always find plenty of talkers. The young girls themselves, I believe, like me very much; and as for me, I delight in the young girls. They are often very pretty; not so pretty as people say in the magazines, but pretty enough. The magazines rather overdo that; they make a mistake. I have seen no great beauties, but the level of prettiness is high, and occasionally one sees a woman completely handsome. (As a general thing, a pretty person here means a person with a pretty face. The figure is rarely mentioned, though there are several good ones.) The level of prettiness is high, but the level of conversation is low; that's one of the signs of its being a young ladies' country. There are a good many things young ladies can't talk about; but think of all the things they can, when they are as clever as most of these. Perhaps one ought to content one's self with that measure, but it's difficult if one has lived for a while by a larger one. This one is decidedly narrow; I stretch it sometimes till it cracks. Then it is that they call me coarse, which I undoubtedly am, thank Heaven! People's talk is of course much more chatiee over here than in Europe; I am struck with that wherever I go. There are certain things that are never said at all, certain allusions that are never made. There are no light stories, no propos risques. I don't know exactly what people talk about, for the supply of scandal is small, and it's poor in quality. They don't seem, however, to lack topics. The young girls are always there; they keep the gates of conversation; very little passes that is not innocent. I find we do very well without wickedness; and, for myself, as I take my ease, I don't miss my liberties. You remember what I thought of the tone of your table in Florence, and how surprised you were when I asked you why you allowed such things. You said they were like the courses of the seasons; one couldn't prevent them; also that to change the tone of your table you would have to change so many other things. Of course, in your house one never saw a young girl; I was the only spinster, and no one was afraid of me! Of course, too, if talk is more innocent in this country, manners are so, to begin with. The liberty of the young people is the strongest proof of it. The young girls are let loose in the world, and the world gets more good of it than ces demoiselles get harm. In your world--excuse me, but you know what I mean--this wouldn't do at all. Your world is a sad affair, and the young ladies would encounter all sorts of horrors. Over here, considering the way they knock about, they remain wonderfully simple, and the reason is that society protects them instead of setting them traps. There is almost no gallantry, as you understand it; the flirtations are child's play. People have no time for making love; the men, in particular, are extremely busy. I am told that sort of thing consumes hours; I have never had any time for it myself. If the leisure class should increase here considerably, there may possibly be a change; but I doubt it, for the women seem to me in all essentials exceedingly reserved. Great superficial frankness, but an extreme dread of complications. The men strike me as very good fellows. I think that at bottom they are better than the women, who are very subtle, but rather hard. They are not so nice to the men as the men are to them; I mean, of course, in proportion, you know. But women are not so nice as men, "anyhow," as they say here. The men, of course, are professional, commercial; there are very few gentlemen pure and simple. This personage needs to be very well done, however, to be of great utility; and I suppose you won't pretend that he is always well done in your countries. When he's not, the less of him the better. It's very much the same, however, with the system on which the young girls in this country are brought up. (You see, I have to come back to the young girls.) When it succeeds, they are the most charming possible; when it doesn't, the failure is disastrous. If a girl is a very nice girl, the American method brings her to great completeness--makes all her graces flower; but if she isn't nice, it makes her exceedingly disagreeable--elaborately and fatally perverts her. In a word, the American girl is rarely negative, and when she isn't a great success she is a great warning. In nineteen cases out of twenty, among the people who know how to live--I won't say what THEIR proportion is-- the results are highly satisfactory. The girls are not shy, but I don't know why they should be, for there is really nothing here to be afraid of. Manners are very gentle, very humane; the democratic system deprives people of weapons that every one doesn't equally possess. No one is formidable; no one is on stilts; no one has great pretensions or any recognised right to be arrogant. I think there is not much wickedness, and there is certainly less cruelty than with you. Every one can sit: no one is kept standing. One is much less liable to be snubbed, which you will say is a pity. I think it is to a certain extent; but, on the other hand, folly is less fatuous, in form, than in your countries; and as people generally have fewer revenges to take, there is less need of their being stamped on in advance. The general good nature, the social equality, deprive them of triumphs on the one hand, and of grievances on the other. There is extremely little impertinence; there is almost none. You will say I am describing a terrible society,--a society without great figures or great social prizes. You have hit it, my dear; there are no great figures. (The great prize, of course, in Europe, is the opportunity to be a great figure.) You would miss these things a good deal,--you who delight to contemplate greatness; and my advice to you, of course, is never to come back. You would miss the small people even more than the great; every one is middle-sized, and you can never have that momentary sense of tallness which is so agreeable in Europe. There are no brilliant types; the most important people seem to lack dignity. They are very bourgeois; they make little jokes; on occasion they make puns; they have no form; they are too good- natured. The men have no style; the women, who are fidgety and talk too much, have it only in their coiffure, where they have it superabundantly. But I console myself with the greater bonhomie. Have you ever arrived at an English country-house in the dusk of a winter's day? Have you ever made a call in London, when you knew nobody but the hostess? People here are more expressive, more demonstrative and it is a pleasure, when one comes back (if one happens, like me, to be no one in particular), to feel one's social value rise. They attend to you more; they have you on their mind; they talk to you; they listen to you. That is, the men do; the women listen very little--not enough. They interrupt; they talk too much; one feels their presence too much as a sound. I imagine it is partly because their wits are quick, and they think of a good many things to say; not that they always say such wonders. Perfect repose, after all, is not ALL self-control; it is also partly stupidity. American women, however, make too many vague exclamations--say too many indefinite things. In short, they have a great deal of nature. On the whole, I find very little affectation, though we shall probably have more as we improve. As yet, people haven't the assurance that carries those things off; they know too much about each other. The trouble is that over here we have all been brought up together. You will think this a picture of a dreadfully insipid society; but I hasten to add that it's not all so tame as that. I have been speaking of the people that one meets socially; and these are the smallest part of American life. The others--those one meets on a basis of mere convenience--are much more exciting; they keep one's temper in healthy exercise. I mean the people in the shops, and on the railroads; the servants, the hackmen, the labourers, every one of whom you buy anything or have occasion to make an inquiry. With them you need all your best manners, for you must always have enough for two. If you think we are TOO democratic, taste a little of American life in these walks, and you will be reassured. This is the region of inequality, and you will find plenty of people to make your courtesy to. You see it from below--the weight of inequality is on your own back. You asked me to tell you about prices; they are simply dreadful.

IV. FROM THE HONOURABLE EDWARD ANTROBUS, M.P., IN BOSTON, TO THE HONOURABLE MRS. ANTROBUS.

October 17.

My Dear Susan--I sent you a post-card on the 13th and a native newspaper yesterday; I really have had no time to write. I sent you the newspaper partly because it contained a report--extremely incorrect--of some remarks I made at the meeting of the Association of the Teachers of New England; partly because it is so curious that I thought it would interest you and the children. I cut out some portions which I didn't think it would be well for the children to see; the parts remaining contain the most striking features. Please point out to the children the peculiar orthography, which probably will be adopted in England by the time they are grown up; the amusing oddities of expression, etc. Some of them are intentional; you will have heard of the celebrated American humour, etc. (remind me, by the way, on my return to Thistleton, to give you a few examples of it); others are unconscious, and are perhaps on that account the more diverting. Point out to the children the difference (in so far as you are sure that you yourself perceive it). You must excuse me if these lines are not very legible; I am writing them by the light of a railway lamp, which rattles above my left ear; it being only at odd moments that I can find time to look into everything that I wish to. You will say that this is a very odd moment, indeed, when I tell you that I am in bed in a sleeping- car. I occupy the upper berth (I will explain to you the arrangement when I return), while the lower forms the couch--the jolts are fearful--of an unknown female. You will be very anxious for my explanation; but I assure you that it is the custom of the country. I myself am assured that a lady may travel in this manner all over the Union (the Union of States) without a loss of consideration. In case of her occupying the upper berth I presume it would be different; but I must make inquiries on this point. Whether it be the fact that a mysterious being of another sex has retired to rest behind the same curtains, or whether it be the swing of the train, which rushes through the air with very much the same movement as the tail of a kite, the situation is, at any rate, so anomalous that I am unable to sleep. A ventilator is open just over my head, and a lively draught, mingled with a drizzle of cinders, pours in through this ingenious orifice. (I will describe to you its form on my return.) If I had occupied the lower berth I should have had a whole window to myself, and by drawing back the blind (a safe proceeding at the dead of night), I should have been able, by the light of an extraordinary brilliant moon, to see a little better what I write. The question occurs to me, however,--Would the lady below me in that case have ascended to the upper berth? (You know my old taste for contingent inquiries.) I incline to think (from what I have seen) that she would simply have requested me to evacuate my own couch. (The ladies in this country ask for anything they want.) In this case, I suppose, I should have had an extensive view of the country, which, from what I saw of it before I turned in (while the lady beneath me was going to bed), offered a rather ragged expanse, dotted with little white wooden houses, which looked in the moonshine like pasteboard boxes. I have been unable to ascertain as precisely as I should wish by whom these modest residences are occupied; for they are too small to be the homes of country gentlemen, there is no peasantry here, and (in New England, for all the corn comes from the far West) there are no yeomen nor farmers. The information that one receives in this country is apt to be rather conflicting, but I am determined to sift the mystery to the bottom. I have already noted down a multitude of facts bearing upon the points that interest me most--the operation of the school- boards, the co-education of the sexes, the elevation of the tone of the lower classes, the participation of the latter in political life. Political life, indeed, is almost wholly confined to the lower middle class, and the upper section of the lower class. In some of the large towns, indeed, the lowest order of all participates considerably--a very interesting phrase, to which I shall give more attention. It is very gratifying to see the taste for public affairs pervading so many social strata; but the indifference of the gentry is a fact not to be lightly considered. It may be objected, indeed, that there are no gentry; and it is very true that I have not yet encountered a character of the type of Lord Bottomley,--a type which I am free to confess I should be sorry to see disappear from our English system, if system it may be called, where so much is the growth of blind and incoherent forces. It is nevertheless obvious that an idle and luxurious class exists in this country, and that it is less exempt than in our own from the reproach of preferring inglorious ease to the furtherance of liberal ideas. It is rapidly increasing, and I am not sure that the indefinite growth of the dilettante spirit, in connection with large and lavishly-expended wealth, is an unmixed good, even in a society in which freedom of development has obtained so many interesting triumphs. The fact that this body is not represented in the governing class, is perhaps as much the result of the jealousy with which it is viewed by the more earnest workers as of its own--I dare not, perhaps, apply a harsher term than--levity. Such, at least, is the impression I have gathered in the Middle States and in New England; in the South-west, the North-west, and the far West, it will doubtless be liable to correction. These divisions are probably new to you; but they are the general denomination of large and flourishing communities, with which I hope to make myself at least superficially acquainted. The fatigue of traversing, as I habitually do, three or four hundred miles at a bound, is, of course, considerable; but there is usually much to inquire into by the way. The conductors of the trains, with whom I freely converse, are often men of vigorous and original minds, and even of some social eminence. One of them, a few days ago, gave me a letter of introduction to his brother-in-law, who is president of a Western University. Don't have any fear, therefore, that I am not in the best society! The arrangements for travelling are, as a general thing, extremely ingenious, as you will probably have inferred from what I told you above; but it must at the same time be conceded that some of them are more ingenious than happy. Some of the facilities, with regard to luggage, the transmission of parcels, etc., are doubtless very useful when explained, but I have not yet succeeded in mastering the intricacies. There are, on the other hand, no cabs and no porters, and I have calculated that I have myself carried my impedimenta--which, you know, are somewhat numerous, and from which I cannot bear to be separated--some seventy, or eighty miles. I have sometimes thought it was a great mistake not to bring Plummeridge; he would have been useful on such occasions. On the other hand, the startling question would have presented itself--Who would have carried Plummeridge's portmanteau? He would have been useful, indeed, for brushing and packing my clothes, and getting me my tub; I travel with a large tin one--there are none to be obtained at the inns--and the transport of this receptacle often presents the most insoluble difficulties. It is often, too, an object of considerable embarrassment in arriving at private houses, where the servants have less reserve of manner than in England; and to tell you the truth, I am by no means certain at the present moment that the tub has been placed in the train with me. "On board" the train is the consecrated phrase here; it is an allusion to the tossing and pitching of the concatenation of cars, so similar to that of a vessel in a storm. As I was about to inquire, however, Who would get Plummeridge HIS tub, and attend to his little comforts? We could not very well make our appearance, on coming to stay with people, with TWO of the utensils I have named; though, as regards a single one, I have had the courage, as I may say, of a life-long habit. It would hardly be expected that we should both use the same; though there have been occasions in my travels, as to which I see no way of blinking the fact, that Plummeridge would have had to sit down to dinner with me. Such a contingency would completely have unnerved him; and, on the whole, it was doubtless the wiser part to leave him respectfully touching his hat on the tender in the Mersey. No one touches his hat over here, and though it is doubtless the sign of a more advanced social order, I confess that when I see poor Plummeridge again, this familiar little gesture-- familiar, I mean, only in the sense of being often seen--will give me a measurable satisfaction. You will see from what I tell you that democracy is not a mere word in this country, and I could give you many more instances of its universal reign. This, however, is what we come here to look at, and, in so far as there seems to be proper occasion, to admire; though I am by no means sure that we can hope to establish within an appreciable time a corresponding change in the somewhat rigid fabric of English manners. I am not even prepared to affirm that such a change is desirable; you know this is one of the points on which I do not as yet see my way to going as far as Lord B-- . I have always held that there is a certain social ideal of inequality as well as of equality, and if I have found the people of this country, as a general thing, quite equal to each other, I am not sure that I am prepared to go so far as to say that, as a whole, they are equal to--excuse that dreadful blot! The movement of the train and the precarious nature of the light--it is close to my nose, and most offensive--would, I flatter myself, long since have got the better of a less resolute diarist! What I was not prepared for was the very considerable body of aristocratic feeling that lurks beneath this republican simplicity. I have on several occasions been made the confidant of these romantic but delusive vagaries, of which the stronghold appears to be the Empire City,--a slang name for New York. I was assured in many quarters that that locality, at least, is ripe for a monarchy, and if one of the Queen's sons would come and talk it over, he would meet with the highest encouragement. This information was given me in strict confidence, with closed doors, as it were; it reminded me a good deal of the dreams of the old Jacobites, when they whispered their messages to the king across the water. I doubt, however, whether these less excusable visionaries will be able to secure the services of a Pretender, for I fear that in such a case he would encounter a still more fatal Culloden. I have given a good deal of time, as I told you, to the educational system, and have visited no fewer than one hundred and forty--three schools and colleges. It is extraordinary, the number of persons who are being educated in this country; and yet, at the same time, the tone of the people is less scholarly than one might expect. A lady, a few days since, described to me her daughter as being always "on the go," which I take to be a jocular way of saying that the young lady was very fond of paying visits. Another person, the wife of a United States senator, informed me that if I should go to Washington in January, I should be quite "in the swim." I inquired the meaning of the phrase, but her explanation made it rather more than less ambiguous. To say that I am on the go describes very accurately my own situation. I went yesterday to the Pognanuc High School, to hear fifty-seven boys and girls recite in unison a most remarkable ode to the American flag, and shortly afterward attended a ladies' lunch, at which some eighty or ninety of the sex were present. There was only one individual in trousers--his trousers, by the way, though he brought a dozen pair, are getting rather seedy. The men in America do not partake of this meal, at which ladies assemble in large numbers to discuss religions, political, and social topics. These immense female symposia (at which every delicacy is provided) are one of the most striking features of American life, and would seem to prove that men are not so indispensable in the scheme of creation as they sometimes suppose. I have been admitted on the footing of an Englishman--"just to show you some of our bright women," the hostess yesterday remarked. ("Bright" here has the meaning of

INTELLECTUAL.) I perceived, indeed, a great many intellectual foreheads. These curious collations are organised according to age. I have also been present as an inquiring stranger at several "girls' lunches," from which married ladies are rigidly excluded, but where the fair revellers are equally numerous and equally bright. There is a good deal I should like to tell you about my study of the educational question, but my position is somewhat cramped, and I must dismiss it briefly. My leading impression is that the children in this country are better educated than the adults. The position of a child is, on the whole, one of great distinction. There is a popular ballad of which the refrain, if I am not mistaken, is "Make me a child again, just for to-night!" and which seems to express the sentiment of regret for lost privileges. At all events they are a powerful and independent class, and have organs, of immense circulation, in the press. They are often extremely "bright." I have talked with a great many teachers, most of them lady-teachers, as they are called in this country. The phrase does not mean teachers of ladies, as you might suppose, but applies to the sex of the instructress, who often has large classes of young men under her control. I was lately introduced to a young woman of twenty-three, who occupies the chair of Moral Philosophy and Belles-Lettres in a Western college, and who told me with the utmost frankness that she was adored by the undergraduates. This young woman was the daughter of a petty trader in one of the South western States, and had studied at Amanda College, in Missourah, an institution at which young people of the two sexes pursue their education together. She was very pretty and modest, and expressed a great desire to see something of English country life, in consequence of which I made her promise to come down to Thistleton in the event of her crossing the Atlantic. She is not the least like Gwendolen or Charlotte, and I am not prepared to say how they would get on with her; the boys would probably do better. Still, I think her acquaintance would be of value to Miss Bumpus, and the two might pass their time very pleasantly in the school-room. I grant you freely that those I have seen here are much less comfortable than the school-room at Thistleton. Has Charlotte, by the way, designed any more texts for the walls? I have been extremely interested in my visit to Philadelphia, where I saw several thousand little red houses with white steps, occupied by intelligent artizans, and arranged (in streets) on the rectangular system. Improved cooking-stoves, rose-wood pianos, gas, and hot water, aesthetic furniture, and complete sets of the British Essayists. A tramway through every street; every block of equal length; blocks and houses scientifically lettered and numbered. There is absolutely no loss of time, and no need of looking for anything, or, indeed, at anything. The mind always on one's object; it is very delightful.

V. FROM LOUIS LEVERETT, IN BOSTON, TO HARVARD TREMONT, IN PARIS.

November.

The scales have turned, my sympathetic Harvard, and the beam that has lifted you up has dropped me again on this terribly hard spot. I am extremely sorry to have missed you in London, but I received your little note, and took due heed of your injunction to let you know how I got on. I don't get on at all, my dear Harvard--I am consumed with the love of the farther shore. I have been so long away that I have dropped out of my place in this little Boston world, and the shallow tides of New England life have closed over it. I am a stranger here, and I find it hard to believe that I ever was a native. It is very hard, very cold, very vacant. I think of your warm, rich Paris; I think of the Boulevard St. Michel on the mild spring evenings. I see the little corner by the window (of the Cafe de la Jeunesse)--where I used to sit; the doors are open, the soft deep breath of the great city comes in. It is brilliant, yet there is a kind of tone, of body, in the brightness; the mighty murmur of the ripest civilisation in the world comes in; the dear old peuple de Paris, the most interesting people in the world, pass by. I have a little book in my pocket; it is exquisitely printed, a modern Elzevir. It is a lyric cry from the heart of young France, and is full of the sentiment of form. There is no form here, dear Harvard; I had no idea how little form there was. I don't know what I shall do; I feel so un-draped, so uncurtained, so uncushioned; I feel as if I were sitting in the centre of a mighty "reflector." A terrible crude glare is over everything; the earth looks peeled and excoriated; the raw heavens seem to bleed with the quick hard light. I have not got back my rooms in West Cedar Street; they are occupied by a mesmeric healer. I am staying at an hotel, and it is very dreadful. Nothing for one's self; nothing for one's preferences and habits. No one to receive you when you arrive; you push in through a crowd, you edge up to a counter; you write your name in a horrible book, where every one may come and stare at it and finger it. A man behind the counter stares at you in silence; his stare seems to say to you, "What the devil do YOU want?" But after this stare he never looks at you again. He tosses down a key at you; he presses a bell; a savage Irishman arrives. "Take him away," he seems to say to the Irishman; but it is all done in silence; there is no answer to your own speech,--"What is to be done with me, please?" "Wait and you will see," the awful silence seems to say. There is a great crowd around you, but there is also a great stillness; every now and then you hear some one expectorate. There are a thousand people in this huge and hideous structure; they feed together in a big white-walled room. It is lighted by a thousand gas-jets, and heated by cast-iron screens, which vomit forth torrents of scorching air. The temperature is terrible; the atmosphere is more so; the furious light and heat seem to intensify the dreadful definiteness. When things are so ugly, they should not be so definite; and they are terribly ugly here. There is no mystery in the corners; there is no light and shade in the types. The people are haggard and joyless; they look as if they had no passions, no tastes, no senses. They sit feeding in silence, in the dry hard light; occasionally I hear the high firm note of a child. The servants are black and familiar; their faces shine as they shuffle about; there are blue tones in their dark masks. They have no manners; they address you, but they don't answer you; they plant themselves at your elbow (it rubs their clothes as you eat), and watch you as if your proceedings were strange. They deluge you with iced water; it's the only thing they will bring you; if you look round to summon them, they have gone for more. If you read the newspaper--which I don't, gracious Heaven! I can't--they hang over your shoulder and peruse it also. I always fold it up and present it to them; the newspapers here are indeed for an African taste. There are long corridors defended by gusts of hot air; down the middle swoops a pale little girl on parlour skates. "Get out of my way!" she shrieks as she passes; she has ribbons in her hair and frills on her dress; she makes the tour of the immense hotel. I think of Puck, who put a girdle round the earth in forty minutes, and wonder what he said as he flitted by. A black waiter marches past me, bearing a tray, which he thrusts into my spine as he goes. It is laden with large white jugs; they tinkle as he moves, and I recognise the unconsoling fluid. We are dying of iced water, of hot air, of gas. I sit in my room thinking of these things--this room of mine which is a chamber of pain. The walls are white and bare, they shine in the rays of a horrible chandelier of imitation bronze, which depends from the middle of the ceiling. It flings a patch of shadow on a small table covered with white marble, of which the genial surface supports at the present moment the sheet of paper on which I address you; and when I go to bed (I like to read in bed, Harvard) it becomes an object of mockery and torment. It dangles at inaccessible heights; it stares me in the face; it flings the light upon the covers of my book, but not upon the page-- the little French Elzevir that I love so well. I rise and put out the gas, and then my room becomes even lighter than before. Then a crude illumination from the hall, from the neighbouring room, pours through the glass openings that surmount the two doors of my apartment. It covers my bed, where I toss and groan; it beats in through my closed lids; it is accompanied by the most vulgar, though the most human, sounds. I spring up to call for some help, some remedy; but there is no bell, and I feel desolate and weak. There is only a strange orifice in the wall, through which the traveller in distress may transmit his appeal. I fill it with incoherent sounds, and sounds more incoherent yet come back to me. I gather at last their meaning; they appear to constitute a somewhat stern inquiry. A hollow impersonal voice wishes to know what I want, and the very question paralyses me. I want everything--yet I want nothing--nothing this hard impersonality can give! I want my little corner of Paris; I want the rich, the deep, the dark Old World; I want to be out of this horrible place. Yet I can't confide all this to that mechanical tube; it would be of no use; a mocking laugh would come up from the office. Fancy appealing in these sacred, these intimate moments, to an "office"; fancy calling out into indifferent space for a candle, for a curtain! I pay incalculable sums in this dreadful house, and yet I haven't a servant to wait upon me. I fling myself back on my couch, and for a long time afterward the orifice in the wall emits strange murmurs and rumblings. It seems unsatisfied, indignant; it is evidently scolding me for my vagueness. My vagueness, indeed, dear Harvard! I loathe their horrible arrangements; isn't that definite enough? You asked me to tell you whom I see, and what I think of my friends. I haven't very many; I don't feel at all en rapport. The people are very good, very serious, very devoted to their work; but there is a terrible absence of variety of type. Every one is Mr. Jones, Mr. Brown; and every one looks like Mr. Jones and Mr. Brown. They are thin; they are diluted in the great tepid bath of Democracy! They lack completeness of identity; they are quite without modelling. No, they are not beautiful, my poor Harvard; it must be whispered that they are not beautiful. You may say that they are as beautiful as the French, as the Germans; but I can't agree with you there. The French, the Germans, have the greatest beauty of all--the beauty of their ugliness--the beauty of the strange, the grotesque. These people are not even ugly; they are only plain. Many of the girls are pretty; but to be only pretty is (to my sense) to be plain. Yet I have had some talk. I have seen a woman. She was on the steamer, and I afterward saw her in New York--a peculiar type, a real personality; a great deal of modelling, a great deal of colour, and yet a great deal of mystery. She was not, however, of this country; she was a compound of far-off things. But she was looking for something here--like me. We found each other, and for a moment that was enough. I have lost her now; I am sorry, because she liked to listen to me. She has passed away; I shall not see her again. She liked to listen to me; she almost understood!

VI. FROM M. GUSTAVE LEJAUNE, OF THE FRENCH ACADEMY, TO M. ADOLPHE BOUCHE, IN PARIS.

Washington, October 5.

I give you my little notes; you must make allowances for haste, for bad inns, for the perpetual scramble, for ill-humour. Everywhere the same impression--the platitude of unbalanced democracy intensified by the platitude of the spirit of commerce. Everything on an immense scale--everything illustrated by millions of examples. My brother-in-law is always busy; he has appointments, inspections, interviews, disputes. The people, it appears, are incredibly sharp in conversation, in argument; they wait for you in silence at the corner of the road, and then they suddenly discharge their revolver. If you fall, they empty your pockets; the only chance is to shoot them first. With that, no amenities, no preliminaries, no manners, no care for the appearance. I wander about while my brother is occupied; I lounge along the streets; I stop at the corners; I look into the shops; je regarde passer les femmes. It's an easy country to see; one sees everything there is; the civilisation is skin deep; you don't have to dig. This positive, practical, pushing bourgeoisie is always about its business; it lives in the street, in the hotel, in the train; one is always in a crowd--there are seventy-five people in the tramway. They sit in your lap; they stand on your toes; when they wish to pass they simply push you. Everything in silence; they know that silence is golden, and they have the worship of gold. When the conductor wishes your fare he gives you a poke, very serious, without a word. As for the types-- but there is only one--they are all variations of the same--the commis-voyageur minus the gaiety. The women are often pretty; you meet the young ones in the streets, in the trains, in search of a husband. They look at you frankly, coldly, judicially, to see if you will serve; but they don't want what you might think (du moins on me l'assure); they only want the husband. A Frenchman may mistake; he needs to be sure he is right, and I always make sure. They begin at fifteen; the mother sends them out; it lasts all day (with an interval for dinner at a pastry-cook's); sometimes it goes on for ten years. If they haven't found the husband then, they give it up; they make place for the cadettes, as the number of women is enormous. No salons, no society, no conversation; people don't receive at home; the young girls have to look for the husband where they can. It is no disgrace not to find him--several have never done so. They continue to go about unmarried--from the force of habit, from the love of movement, without hopes, without regret--no imagination, no sensibility, no desire for the convent. We have made several journeys--few of less than three hundred miles. Enormous trains, enormous waggons, with beds and lavatories, and negroes who brush you with a big broom, as if they were grooming a horse. A bounding movement, a roaring noise, a crowd of people who look horribly tired, a boy who passes up and down throwing pamphlets and sweetmeats into your lap--that is an American journey. There are windows in the waggons--enormous, like everything else; but there is nothing to see. The country is a void--no features, no objects, no details, nothing to show you that you are in one place more than another. Aussi, you are not in one place, you are everywhere, anywhere; the train goes a hundred miles an hour. The cities are all the same; little houses ten feet high, or else big ones two hundred; tramways, telegraph-poles, enormous signs, holes in the pavement, oceans of mud, commis-voyageurs, young ladies looking for the husband. On the other hand, no beggars and no cocottes--none, at least, that you see. A colossal mediocrity, except (my brother-in-law tells me) in the machinery, which is magnificent. Naturally, no architecture (they make houses of wood and of iron), no art, no literature, no theatre. I have opened some of the books; mais ils ne se laissent pas lire. No form, no matter, no style, no general ideas! they seem to be written for children and young ladies. The most successful (those that they praise most) are the facetious; they sell in thousands of editions. I have looked into some of the most vantes; but you need to be forewarned, to know that they are amusing; des plaisanteries de croquemort. They have a novelist with pretensions to literature, who writes about the chase for the husband and the adventures of the rich Americans in our corrupt old Europe, where their primaeval candour puts the Europeans to shame. C'est proprement ecrit; but it's terribly pale. What isn't pale is the newspapers--enormous, like everything else (fifty columns of advertisements), and full of the commerages of a continent. And such a tone, grand Dieu! The amenities, the personalities, the recriminations, are like so many coups de revolver. Headings six inches tall; correspondences from places one never heard of; telegrams from Europe about Sarah Bernhardt; little paragraphs about nothing at all; the menu of the neighbour's dinner; articles on the European situation a pouffer de rire; all the tripotage of local politics. The reportage is incredible; I am chased up and down by the interviewers. The matrimonial infelicities of M. and Madame X. (they give the name), tout au long, with every detail--not in six lines, discreetly veiled, with an art of insinuation, as with us; but with all the facts (or the fictions), the letters, the dates, the places, the hours. I open a paper at hazard, and I find au beau milieu, a propos of nothing, the announcement--"Miss Susan Green has the longest nose in Western New York." Miss Susan Green (je me renseigne) is a celebrated authoress; and the Americans have the reputation of spoiling their women. They spoil them a coups de poing. We have seen few interiors (no one speaks French); but if the newspapers give an idea of the domestic moeurs, the moeurs must be curious. The passport is abolished, but they have printed my signalement in these sheets,-- perhaps for the young ladies who look for the husband. We went one night to the theatre; the piece was French (they are the only ones), but the acting was American--too American; we came out in the middle. The want of taste is incredible. An Englishman whom I met tells me that even the language corrupts itself from day to day; an Englishman ceases to understand. It encourages me to find that I am not the only one. There are things every day that one can't describe. Such is Washington, where we arrived this morning, coming from Philadelphia. My brother-in-law wishes to see the Bureau of Patents, and on our arrival he went to look at his machines, while I walked about the streets and visited the Capitol! The human machine is what interests me most. I don't even care for the political--for that's what they call their Government here--"the machine." It operates very roughly, and some day, evidently, it will explode. It is true that you would never suspect that they have a government; this is the principal seat, but, save for three or four big buildings, most of them affreux, it looks like a settlement of negroes. No movement, no officials, no authority, no embodiment of the state. Enormous streets, comme toujours, lined with little red houses where nothing ever passes but the tramway. The Capitol--a vast structure, false classic, white marble, iron and stucco, which has assez grand air--must be seen to be appreciated. The goddess of liberty on the top, dressed in a bear's skin; their liberty over here is the liberty of bears. You go into the Capitol as you would into a railway station; you walk about as you would in the Palais Royal. No functionaries, no door-keepers, no officers, no uniforms, no badges, no restrictions, no authority--nothing but a crowd of shabby people circulating in a labyrinth of spittoons. We are too much governed, perhaps, in France; but at least we have a certain incarnation of the national conscience, of the national dignity. The dignity is absent here, and I am told that the conscience is an abyss. "L'etat c'est moi" even--I like that better than the spittoons. These implements are architectural, monumental; they are the only monuments. En somme, the country is interesting, now that we too have the Republic; it is the biggest illustration, the biggest warning. It is the last word of democracy, and that word is--flatness. It is very big, very rich, and perfectly ugly. A Frenchman couldn't live here; for life with us, after all, at the worst is a sort of appreciation. Here, there is nothing to appreciate. As for the people, they are the English MINUS the conventions. You can fancy what remains. The women, pourtant, are sometimes--rather well turned. There was one at Philadelphia--I made her acquaintance by accident--whom it is probable I shall see again. She is not looking for the husband; she has already got one. It was at the hotel; I think the husband doesn't matter. A Frenchman, as I have said, may mistake, and he needs to be sure he is right. Aussi, I always make sure!

VII. FROM MARCELLUS COCKEREL, IN WASHINGTON, TO MRS. COOLER, NEE COCKEREL, AT OAKLAND, CALIFORNIA.

October 25.

I ought to have written to you long before this, for I have had your last excellent letter for four months in my hands. The first half of that time I was still in Europe; the last I have spent on my native soil. I think, therefore, my silence is owing to the fact that over there I was too miserable to write, and that here I have been too happy. I got back the 1st of September--you will have seen it in the papers. Delightful country, where one sees everything in the papers--the big, familiar, vulgar, good-natured, delightful papers, none of which has any reputation to keep up for anything but getting the news! I really think that has had as much to do as anything else with my satisfaction at getting home--the difference in what they call the "tone of the press." In Europe it's too dreary--the sapience, the solemnity, the false respectability, the verbosity, the long disquisitions on superannuated subjects. Here the newspapers are like the railroad trains, which carry everything that comes to the station, and have only the religion of punctuality. As a woman, however, you probably detest them; you think they are (the great word) vulgar. I admitted it just now, and I am very happy to have an early opportunity to announce to you that that idea has quite ceased to have any terrors for me. There are some conceptions to which the female mind can never rise. Vulgarity is a stupid, superficial, question-begging accusation, which has become today the easiest refuge of mediocrity. Better than anything else, it saves people the trouble of thinking, and anything which does that, succeeds. You must know that in these last three years in Europe I have become terribly vulgar myself; that's one service my travels have rendered me. By three years in Europe I mean three years in foreign parts altogether, for I spent several months of that time in Japan, India, and the rest of the East. Do you remember when you bade me good-bye in San Francisco, the night before I embarked for Yokohama? You foretold that I should take such a fancy to foreign life that America would never see me more, and that if YOU should wish to see me (an event you were good enough to regard as possible), you would have to make a rendezvous in Paris or in Rome. I think we made one (which you never kept), but I shall never make another for those cities. It was in Paris, however, that I got your letter; I remember the moment as well as if it were (to my honour) much more recent. You must know that, among many places I dislike, Paris carries the palm. I am bored to death there; it's the home of every humbug. The life is full of that false comfort which is worse than discomfort, and the small, fat, irritable people, give me the shivers. I had been making these reflections even more devoutly than usual one very tiresome evening toward the beginning of last summer, when, as I re-entered my hotel at ten o'clock, the little reptile of a portress handed me your gracious lines. I was in a villainous humour. I had been having an over- dressed dinner in a stuffy restaurant, and had gone from there to a suffocating theatre, where, by way of amusement, I saw a play in which blood and lies were the least of the horrors. The theatres over there are insupportable; the atmosphere is pestilential. People sit with their elbows in your sides; they squeeze past you every half-hour. It was one of my bad moments; I have a great many in Europe. The conventional perfunctory play, all in falsetto, which I seemed to have seen a thousand times; the horrible faces of the people; the pushing, bullying ouvreuse, with her false politeness, and her real rapacity, drove me out of the place at the end of an hour; and, as it was too early to go home, I sat down before a cafe on the Boulevard, where they served me a glass of sour, watery beer. There on the Boulevard, in the summer night, life itself was even uglier than the play, and it wouldn't do for me to tell you what I saw. Besides, I was sick of the Boulevard, with its eternal grimace, and the deadly sameness of the article de Paris, which pretends to be so various--the shop-windows a wilderness of rubbish, and the passers-by a procession of manikins. Suddenly it came over me that I was supposed to be amusing myself-- my face was a yard long--and that you probably at that moment were saying to your husband: "He stays away so long! What a good time he must be having!" The idea was the first thing that had made me smile for a month; I got up and walked home, reflecting, as I went, that I was "seeing Europe," and that, after all, one MUST see Europe. It was because I had been convinced of this that I came out, and it is because the operation has been brought to a close that I have been so happy for the last eight weeks. I was very conscientious about it, and, though your letter that night made me abominably homesick, I held out to the end, knowing it to be once for all. I sha'n't trouble Europe again; I shall see America for the rest of my days. My long delay has had the advantage that now, at least, I can give you my impressions--I don't mean of Europe; impressions of Europe are easy to get--but of this country, as it strikes the re-instated exile. Very likely you'll think them queer; but keep my letter, and twenty years hence they will be quite commonplace. They won't even be vulgar. It was very deliberate, my going round the world. I knew that one ought to see for one's self, and that I should have eternity, so to speak, to rest. I travelled energetically; I went everywhere and saw everything; took as many letters as possible, and made as many acquaintances. In short, I held my nose to the grindstone. The upshot of it all is that I have got rid of a superstition. We have so many, that one the less-- perhaps the biggest of all--makes a real difference in one's comfort. The superstition in question--of course you have it--is that there is no salvation but through Europe. Our salvation is here, if we have eyes to see it, and the salvation of Europe into the bargain; that is, if Europe is to be saved, which I rather doubt. Of course you'll call me a bird of freedom, a braggart, a waver of the stars and stripes; but I'm in the delightful position of not minding in the least what any one calls me. I haven't a mission; I don't want to preach; I have simply arrived at a state of mind; I have got Europe off my back. You have no idea how it simplifies things, and how jolly it makes me feel. Now I can live; now I can talk. If we wretched Americans could only say once for all, "Oh, Europe be hanged!" we should attend much better to our proper business. We have simply to live our life, and the rest will look after itself. You will probably inquire what it is that I like better over here, and I will answer that it's simply--life. Disagreeables for disagreeables, I prefer our own. The way I have been bored and bullied in foreign parts, and the way I have had to say I found it pleasant! For a good while this appeared to be a sort of congenital obligation, but one fine day it occurred to me that there was no obligation at all, and that it would ease me immensely to admit to myself that (for me, at least) all those things had no importance. I mean the things they rub into you in Europe; the tiresome international topics, the petty politics, the stupid social customs, the baby-house scenery. The vastness and freshness of this American world, the great scale and great pace of our development, the good sense and good nature of the people, console me for there being no cathedrals and no Titians. I hear nothing about Prince Bismarck and Gambetta, about the Emperor William and the Czar of Russia, about Lord Beaconsfield and the Prince of Wales. I used to get so tired of their Mumbo-Jumbo of a Bismarck, of his secrets and surprises, his mysterious intentions and oracular words. They revile us for our party politics; but what are all the European jealousies and rivalries, their armaments and their wars, their rapacities and their mutual lies, but the intensity of the spirit of party? what question, what interest, what idea, what need of mankind, is involved in any of these things? Their big, pompous armies, drawn up in great silly rows, their gold lace, their salaams, their hierarchies, seem a pastime for children; there's a sense of humour and of reality over here that laughs at all that. Yes, we are nearer the reality--we are nearer what they will all have to come to. The questions of the future are social questions, which the Bismarcks and Beaconsfields are very much afraid to see settled; and the sight of a row of supercilious potentates holding their peoples like their personal property, and bristling all over, to make a mutual impression, with feathers and sabres, strikes us as a mixture of the grotesque and the abominable. What do we care for the mutual impressions of potentates who amuse themselves with sitting on people? Those things are their own affair, and they ought to be shut up in a dark room to have it out together. Once one feels, over here, that the great questions of the future are social questions, that a mighty tide is sweeping the world to democracy, and that this country is the biggest stage on which the drama can be enacted, the fashionable European topics seem petty and parochial. They talk about things that we have settled ages ago, and the solemnity with which they propound to you their little domestic embarrassments makes a heavy draft on one's good nature. In England they were talking about the Hares and Rabbits Bill, about the extension of the County Franchise, about the Dissenters' Burials, about the Deceased Wife's Sister, about the abolition of the House of Lords, about heaven knows what ridiculous little measure for the propping-up of their ridiculous little country. And they call US provincial! It is hard to sit and look respectable while people discuss the utility of the House of Lords, and the beauty of a State Church, and it's only in a dowdy musty civilisation that you'll find them doing such things. The lightness and clearness of the social air, that's the great relief in these parts. The gentility of bishops, the propriety of parsons, even the impressiveness of a restored cathedral, give less of a charm to life than that. I used to be furious with the bishops and parsons, with the humbuggery of the whole affair, which every one was conscious of, but which people agreed not to expose, because they would be compromised all round. The convenience of life over here, the quick and simple arrangements, the absence of the spirit of routine, are a blessed change from the stupid stiffness with which I struggled for two long years. There were people with swords and cockades, who used to order me about; for the simplest operation of life I had to kootoo to some bloated official. When it was a question of my doing a little differently from others, the bloated official gasped as if I had given him a blow on the stomach; he needed to take a week to think of it. On the other hand, it's impossible to take an American by surprise; he is ashamed to confess that he has not the wit to do a thing that another man has had the wit to think of. Besides being as good as his neighbour, he must therefore be as clever--which is an affliction only to people who are afraid he may be cleverer. If this general efficiency and spontaneity of the people--the union of the sense of freedom with the love of knowledge--isn't the very essence of a high civilisation, I don't know what a high civilisation is. I felt this greater ease on my first railroad journey--felt the blessing of sitting in a train where I could move about, where I could stretch my legs, and come and go, where I had a seat and a window to myself, where there were chairs, and tables, and food, and drink. The villainous little boxes on the European trains, in which you are stuck down in a corner, with doubled-up knees, opposite to a row of people--often most offensive types, who stare at you for ten hours on end--these were part of my two years' ordeal. The large free way of doing things here is everywhere a pleasure. In London, at my hotel, they used to come to me on Saturday to make me order my Sunday's dinner, and when I asked for a sheet of paper, they put it into the bill. The meagreness, the stinginess, the perpetual expectation of a sixpence, used to exasperate me. Of course, I saw a great many people who were pleasant; but as I am writing to you, and not to one of them, I may say that they were dreadfully apt to be dull. The imagination among the people I see here is more flexible; and then they have the advantage of a larger horizon. It's not bounded on the north by the British aristocracy, and on the south by the scrutin de liste. (I mix up the countries a little, but they are not worth the keeping apart.) The absence of little conventional measurements, of little cut-and-dried judgments, is an immense refreshment. We are more analytic, more discriminating, more familiar with realities. As for manners, there are bad manners everywhere, but an aristocracy is bad manners organised. (I don't mean that they may not be polite among themselves, but they are rude to every one else.) The sight of all these growing millions simply minding their business, is impressive to me,--more so than all the gilt buttons and padded chests of the Old World; and there is a certain powerful type of "practical" American (you'll find him chiefly in the West) who doesn't brag as I do (I'm not practical), but who quietly feels that he has the Future in his vitals--a type that strikes me more than any I met in your favourite countries. Of course you'll come back to the cathedrals and Titians, but there's a thought that helps one to do without them--the thought that though there's an immense deal of plainness, there's little misery, little squalor, little degradation. There is no regular wife-beating class, and there are none of the stultified peasants of whom it takes so many to make a European noble. The people here are more conscious of things; they invent, they act, they answer for themselves; they are not (I speak of social matters) tied up by authority and precedent. We shall have all the Titians by and by, and we shall move over a few cathedrals. You had better stay here if you want to have the best. Of course, I am a roaring Yankee; but you'll call me that if I say the least, so I may as well take my ease, and say the most. Washington's a most entertaining place; and here at least, at the seat of government, one isn't overgoverned. In fact, there's no government at all to speak of; it seems too good to be true. The first day I was here I went to the Capitol, and it took me ever so long to figure to myself that I had as good a right there as any one else--that the whole magnificent pile (it IS magnificent, by the way) was in fact my own. In Europe one doesn't rise to such conceptions, and my spirit had been broken in Europe. The doors were gaping wide--I walked all about; there were no door-keepers, no officers, nor flunkeys--not even a policeman to be seen. It seemed strange not to see a uniform, if only as a patch of colour. But this isn't government by livery. The absence of these things is odd at first; you seem to miss something, to fancy the machine has stopped. It hasn't, though; it only works without fire and smoke. At the end of three days this simple negative impression--the fact is, that there are no soldiers nor spies, nothing but plain black coats--begins to affect the imagination, becomes vivid, majestic, symbolic. It ends by being more impressive than the biggest review I saw in Germany. Of course, I'm a roaring Yankee; but one has to take a big brush to copy a big model. The future is here, of course; but it isn't only that--the present is here as well. You will complain that I don't give you any personal news; but I am more modest for myself than for my country. I spent a month in New York, and while I was there I saw a good deal of a rather interesting girl who came over with me in the steamer, and whom for a day or two I thought I should like to marry. But I shouldn't. She has been spoiled by Europe!

VIII. FROM MISS AURORA CHURCH,
IN NEW YORK, TO MISS WHITESIDE, IN PARIS.

January 9.

I told you (after we landed) about my agreement with mamma--that I was to have my liberty for three months, and if at the end of this time I shouldn't have made a good use of it, I was to give it back to her. Well, the time is up today, and I am very much afraid I haven't made a good use of it. In fact, I haven't made any use of it at all--I haven't got married, for that is what mamma meant by our little bargain. She has been trying to marry me in Europe, for years, without a dot, and as she has never (to the best of my knowledge) even come near it, she thought at last that, if she were to leave it to me, I might do better. I couldn't certainly do worse. Well, my dear, I have done very badly--that is, I haven't done at all. I haven't even tried. I had an idea that this affair came of itself over here; but it hasn't come to me. I won't say I am disappointed, for I haven't, on the whole, seen any one I should like to marry. When you marry people over here, they expect you to love them, and I haven't seen any one I should like to love. I don't know what the reason is, but they are none of them what I have thought of. It may be that I have thought of the impossible; and yet I have seen people in Europe whom I should have liked to marry. It is true, they were almost always married to some one else. What I AM disappointed in is simply having to give back my liberty. I don't wish particularly to be married; and I do wish to do as I like--as I have been doing for the last month. All the same, I am sorry for poor mamma, as nothing has happened that she wished to happen. To begin with, we are not appreciated, not even by the Rucks, who have disappeared, in the strange way in which people over here seem to vanish from the world. We have made no sensation; my new dresses count for nothing (they all have better ones); our philological and historical studies don't show. We have been told we might do better in Boston; but, on the other hand, mamma hears that in Boston the people only marry their cousins. Then mamma is out of sorts because the country is exceedingly dear and we have spent all our money. Moreover, I have neither eloped, nor been insulted, nor been talked about, nor--so far as I know--deteriorated in manners or character; so that mamma is wrong in all her previsions. I think she would have rather liked me to be insulted. But I have been insulted as little as I have been adored. They don't adore you over here; they only make you think they are going to. Do you remember the two gentlemen who were on the ship, and who, after we arrived here, came to see me a tour de role? At first I never dreamed they were making love to me, though mamma was sure it must be that; then, as it went on a good while, I thought perhaps it WAS that; and I ended by seeing that it wasn't anything! It was simply conversation; they are very fond of conversation over here. Mr. Leverett and Mr. Cockerel disappeared one fine day, without the smallest pretension to having broken my heart, I am sure, though it only depended on me to think they had! All the gentlemen are like that; you can't tell what they mean; everything is very confused; society appears to consist of a sort of innocent jilting. I think, on the whole, I AM a little disappointed--I don't mean about one's not marrying; I mean about the life generally. It seems so different at first, that you expect it will be very exciting; and then you find that, after all, when you have walked out for a week or two by yourself, and driven out with a gentleman in a buggy, that's about all there is of it, as they say here. Mamma is very angry at not finding more to dislike; she admitted yesterday that, once one has got a little settled, the country has not even the merit of being hateful. This has evidently something to do with her suddenly proposing three days ago that we should go to the West. Imagine my surprise at such an idea coming from mamma! The people in the pension--who, as usual, wish immensely to get rid of her-- have talked to her about the West, and she has taken it up with a kind of desperation. You see, we must do something; we can't simply remain here. We are rapidly being ruined, and we are not--so to speak--getting married. Perhaps it will be easier in the West; at any rate, it will be cheaper, and the country will have the advantage of being more hateful. It is a question between that and returning to Europe, and for the moment mamma is balancing. I say nothing: I am really indifferent; perhaps I shall marry a pioneer. I am just thinking how I shall give back my liberty. It really won't be possible; I haven't got it any more; I have given it away to others. Mamma may recover it, if she can, from THEM! She comes in at this moment to say that we must push farther--she has decided for the West. Wonderful mamma! It appears that my real chance is for a pioneer--they have sometimes millions. But, fancy us in the West!

The Codes Of Hammurabi And Moses
W. W. Davies

QTY

The discovery of the Hammurabi Code is one of the greatest achievements of archaeology, and is of paramount interest, not only to the student of the Bible, but also to all those interested in ancient history...

Religion   ISBN: *1-59462-338-4*   **Pages:132**
                                              MSRP $12.95

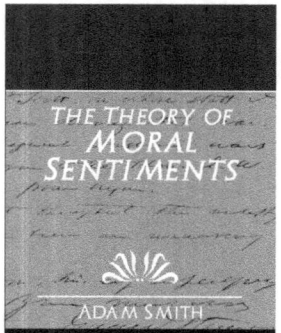

The Theory of Moral Sentiments
Adam Smith

QTY

This work from 1749. contains original theories of conscience amd moral judgment and it is the foundation for systemof morals.

Philosophy   ISBN: *1-59462-777-0*   **Pages:536**
                                              MSRP $19.95

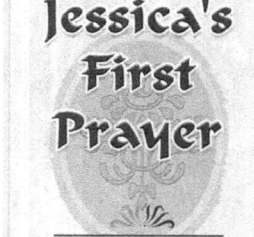

Jessica's First Prayer
Hesba Stretton

QTY

In a screened and secluded corner of one of the many railway-bridges which span the streets of London there could be seen a few years ago, from five o'clock every morning until half past eight, a tidily set-out coffee-stall, consisting of a trestle and board, upon which stood two large tin cans, with a small fire of charcoal burning under each so as to keep the coffee boiling during the early hours of the morning when the work-people were thronging into the city on their way to their daily toil...

Childrens   ISBN: *1-59462-373-2*   **Pages:84**
                                              MSRP $9.95

My Life and Work
Henry Ford

QTY

Henry Ford revolutionized the world with his implementation of mass production for the Model T automobile. Gain valuable business insight into his life and work with his own auto-biography... "We have only started on our development of our country we have not as yet, with all our talk of wonderful progress, done more than scratch the surface. The progress has been wonderful enough but..."

Biographies/   ISBN: *1-59462-198-5*   **Pages:300**
                                              MSRP $21.95

The Art of Cross-Examination
Francis Wellman

I presume it is the experience of every author, after his first book is published upon an important subject, to be almost overwhelmed with a wealth of ideas and illustrations which could readily have been included in his book, and which to his own mind, at least, seem to make a second edition inevitable. Such certainly was the case with me; and when the first edition had reached its sixth impression in five months, I rejoiced to learn that it seemed to my publishers that the book had met with a sufficiently favorable reception to justify a second and considerably enlarged edition. ..

QTY

Reference **ISBN:** *1-59462-647-2*

Pages:412
MSRP $19.95

On the Duty of Civil Disobedience
Henry David Thoreau

Thoreau wrote his famous essay, On the Duty of Civil Disobedience, as a protest against an unjust but popular war and the immoral but popular institution of slave-owning. He did more than write—he declined to pay his taxes, and was hauled off to gaol in consequence. Who can say how much this refusal of his hastened the end of the war and of s avery ?

QTY

Law **ISBN:** *1-59462-747-9*

Pages:48
MSRP $7.45

Dream Psychology Psychoanalysis for Beginners
Sigmund Freud

Sigmund Freud, born Sigismund Schlomo Freud (May 6, 1856 - September 23, 1939), was a Jewish-Austrian neurologist and psychiatrist who co-founded the psychoanalytic school of psychology. Freud is best known for his theories of the unconscious mind, especially involving the mechanism of repression; his redefinition of sexual desire as mobile and directed towards a wide variety of objects; and his therapeutic techniques, especially his understanding of transference n the therapeutic relationship and the presumed value of dreams as sources of insight into unconscious desires.

QTY

Psychology **ISBN:** *1-59462-905-6*

Pages:196
MSRP $15.45

The Miracle of Right Thought
Orison Swett Marden

Believe with all of your heart that you will do what you were made to do. When the mind has once formed the habit of holding cheerful, happy, prosperous pictures, it will not be easy to form the opposite habit. It does not matter how improbable or how far away this realization may see, or how dark the prospects may be, if we visualize them as best we can, as vividly as possible, hold tenaciously to them and vigorously struggle to attain them, they will gradually become actualized, realized in the life. But a desire, a longing without endeavor, a yearning abandoned or held indifferently will vanish without realization.

QTY

Self Help **ISBN:** *1-59462-644-8*

Pages:360
MSRP $25.45

www.bookjungle.com *email: sales@bookjungle.com fax: 630-214-0564 mail: Book Jungle PO Box 2226 Champaign, IL 61825*

QTY

The Rosicrucian Cosmo-Conception Mystic Christianity by *Max Heindel*   ISBN: *1-59462-188-8*   **$38.95**
The Rosicrucian Cosmo-conception is not dogmatic, neither does it appeal to any other authority than the reason of the student. It is: not controversial, but is: sent forth in the, hope that it may help to clear...   New Age/Religion Pages 646

Abandonment To Divine Providence by *Jean-Pierre de Caussade*   ISBN: *1-59462-228-0*   **$25.95**
"The Rev. Jean Pierre de Caussade was one of the most remarkable spiritual writers of the Society of Jesus in France in the 18th Century. His death took place at Toulouse in 1751. His works have gone through many editions and have been republished...   Inspirational/Religion Pages 400

Mental Chemistry by *Charles Haanel*   ISBN: *1-59462-192-6*   **$23.95**
Mental Chemistry allows the change of material conditions by combining and appropriately utilizing the power of the mind. Much like applied chemistry creates something new and unique out of careful combinations of chemicals the mastery of mental chemistry...   New Age Pages 354

The Letters of Robert Browning and Elizabeth Barret Barrett 1845-1846 vol II   ISBN: *1-59462-193-4*   **$35.95**
by *Robert Browning* and Elizabeth Barrett   Biographies Pages 596

Gleanings In Genesis (volume I) by *Arthur W. Pink*   ISBN: *1-59462-130-6*   **$27.45**
Appropriately has Genesis been termed "the seed plot of the Bible" for in it we have, in germ form, almost all of the great doctrines which are afterwards fully developed in the books of Scripture which follow...   Religion/Inspirational Pages 420

The Master Key by *L. W. de Laurence*   ISBN: *1-59462-001-6*   **$30.95**
In no branch of human knowledge has there been a more lively increase of the spirit of research during the past few years than in the study of Psychology, Concentration and Mental Discipline. The requests for authentic lessons in Thought Control, Mental Discipline and...   New Age/Business Pages 422

The Lesser Key Of Solomon Goetia by *L. W. de Laurence*   ISBN: *1-59462-092-X*   **$9.95**
This translation of the first book of the "Lemegton" which is now for the first time made accessible to students of Talismanic Magic was done, after careful collation and edition, from numerous Ancient Manuscripts in Hebrew, Latin, and French...   New Age/Occult Pages 92

Rubaiyat Of Omar Khayyam by *Edward Fitzgerald*   ISBN:*1-59462-332-5*   **$13.95**
Edward Fitzgerald, whom the world has already learned, in spite of his own efforts to remain within the shadow of anonymity, to look upon as one of the rarest poets of the century, was born at Bredfield, in Suffolk, on the 31st of March, 1809. He was the third son of John Purcell...   Music Pages 172

Ancient Law by *Henry Maine*   ISBN: *1-59462-128-4*   **$29.95**
The chief object of the following pages is to indicate some of the earliest ideas of mankind, as they are reflected in Ancient Law, and to point out the relation of those ideas to modern thought.   Religiom/History Pages 452

Far-Away Stories by *William J. Locke*   ISBN: *1-59462-129-2*   **$19.45**
"Good wine needs no bush, but a collection of mixed vintages does. And this book is just such a collection. Some of the stories I do not want to remain buried for ever in the museum files of dead magazine-numbers an author's not unpardonable vanity..."   Fiction Pages 272

Life of David Crockett by *David Crockett*   ISBN: *1-59462-250-7*   **$27.45**
"Colonel David Crockett was one of the most remarkable men of the times in which he lived. Born in humble life, but gifted with a strong will, an indomitable courage, and unremitting perseverance...   Biographies/New Age Pages 424

Lip-Reading by *Edward Nitchie*   ISBN: *1-59462-206-X*   **$25.95**
Edward B. Nitchie, founder of the New York School for the Hard of Hearing, now the Nitchie School of Lip-Reading, Inc, wrote "LIP-READING Principles and Practice". The development and perfecting of this meritorious work on lip-reading was an undertaking...   How-to Pages 400

A Handbook of Suggestive Therapeutics, Applied Hypnotism, Psychic Science   ISBN: *1-59462-214-0*   **$24.95**
by *Henry Munro*   Health/New Age/Health/Self-help Pages 376

A Doll's House: and Two Other Plays by *Henrik Ibsen*   ISBN: *1-59462-112-8*   **$19.95**
Henrik Ibsen created this classic when in revolutionary 1848 Rome. Introducing some striking concepts in playwriting for the realist genre, this play has been studied the world over.   Fiction/Classics/Plays 308

The Light of Asia by *sir Edwin Arnold*   ISBN: *1-59462-204-3*   **$13.95**
In this poetic masterpiece, Edwin Arnold describes the life and teachings of Buddha. The man who was to become known as Buddha to the world was born as Prince Gautama of India but he rejected the worldly riches and abandoned the reigns of power when... Religion/History/Biographies Pages 170

The Complete Works of Guy de Maupassant by *Guy de Maupassant*   ISBN: *1-59462-157-8*   **$16.95**
"For days and days, nights and nights, I had dreamed of that first kiss which was to consecrate our engagement, and I knew not on what spot I should put my lips..."   Fiction/Classics Pages 240

The Art of Cross-Examination by *Francis L. Wellman*   ISBN: *1-59462-309-0*   **$26.95**
Written by a renowned trial lawyer, Wellman imparts his experience and uses case studies to explain how to use psychology to extract desired information through questioning.   How-to/Science/Reference Pages 408

Answered or Unanswered? by *Louisa Vaughan*   ISBN: *1-59462-248-5*   **$10.95**
Miracles of Faith in China   Religion Pages 112

The Edinburgh Lectures on Mental Science (1909) by *Thomas*   ISBN: *1-59462-008-3*   **$11.95**
This book contains the substance of a course of lectures recently given by the writer in the Queen Street Hail, Edinburgh. Its purpose is to indicate the Natural Principles governing the relation between Mental Action and Material Conditions...   New Age/Psychology Pages 148

Ayesha by *H. Rider Haggard*   ISBN: *1-59462-301-5*   **$24.95**
Verily and indeed it is the unexpected that happens! Probably if there was one person upon the earth from whom the Editor of this, and of a certain previous history, did not expect to hear again...   Classics Pages 380

Ayala's Angel by *Anthony Trollope*   ISBN: *1-59462-352-X*   **$29.95**
The two girls were both pretty, but Lucy who was twenty-one who supposed to be simple and comparatively unattractive, whereas Ayala was credited, as her Bombwhat romantic name might show, with poetic charm and a taste for romance. Ayala when her father died was nineteen...   Fiction Pages 484

The American Commonwealth by *James Bryce*   ISBN: *1-59462-286-8*   **$34.45**
An interpretation of American democratic political theory. It examines political mechanics and society from the perspective of Scotsman James Bryce   Politics Pages 572

Stories of the Pilgrims by *Margaret P. Pumphrey*   ISBN: *1-59462-116-0*   **$17.95**
This book explores pilgrims religious oppression in England as well as their escape to Holland and eventual crossing to America on the Mayflower, and their early days in New England...   History Pages 268

QTY

The Fasting Cure *by Sinclair Upton*   ISBN: *1-59462-222-1*   **$13.95**
In the Cosmopolitan Magazine for May, 1910, and in the Contemporary Review (London) for April, 1910, I published an article dealing with my experiences in fasting. I have written a great many magazine articles, but never one which attracted so much attention... New Age/Self Help/Health Pages 164

Hebrew Astrology *by Sepharial*   ISBN: *1-59462-308-2*   **$13.45**
In these days of advanced thinking it is a matter of common observation that we have left many of the old landmarks behind and that we are now pressing forward to greater heights and to a wider horizon than that which represented the mind-content of our progenitors... Astrology Pages 144

Thought Vibration or The Law of Attraction in the Thought World   ISBN: *1-59462-127-6*   **$12.95**

by William Walker Atkinson   *Psychology/Religion Pages 144*

Optimism *by Helen Keller*   ISBN: *1-59462-108-X*   **$15.95**
Helen Keller was blind, deaf, and mute since 19 months old, yet famously learned how to overcome these handicaps, communicate with the world, and spread her lectures promoting optimism. An inspiring read for everyone... Biographies/Inspirational Pages 84

Sara Crewe *by Frances Burnett*   ISBN: *1-59462-360-0*   **$9.45**
In the first place, Miss Minchin lived in London. Her home was a large, dull, tall one, in a large, dull square, where all the houses were alike, and all the sparrows were alike, and where all the door-knockers made the same heavy sound... Childrens/Classic Pages 88

The Autobiography of Benjamin Franklin *by Benjamin Franklin*   ISBN: *1-59462-135-7*   **$24.95**
The Autobiography of Benjamin Franklin has probably been more extensively read than any other American historical work, and no other book of its kind has had such ups and downs of fortune. Franklin lived for many years in England, where he was agent... Biographies/History Pages 332

Name	
Email	
Telephone	
Address	
City, State ZIP	

☐ **Credit Card**   ☐ **Check / Money Order**

Credit Card Number	
Expiration Date	
Signature	

Please Mail to: Book Jungle
PO Box 2226
Champaign, IL 61825
or Fax to: 630-214-0564

ORDERING INFORMATION

web: *www.bookjungle.com*
email: *sales@bookjungle.com*
fax: *630-214-0564*
mail: *Book Jungle PO Box 2226 Champaign, IL 61825*
or PayPal *to sales@bookjungle.com*

Please contact us for bulk discounts

DIRECT-ORDER TERMS

**20% Discount if You Order
Two or More Books**
Free Domestic Shipping!
Accepted: Master Card, Visa,
Discover, American Express